FIVE MONTHS AT ANZAC

In 1914 Lieutenant-Colonel Beeston, accompanied by his faithful dog Paddy, was dispatched overseas with the 4th Field Ambulance of the Australian Imperial Force. Chronicling his experiences of the Gallipoli Campaign, he recounts the irrepressible humour of the Australian soldiery, the privations of field life (including ration biscuits so tough that boxes of them proved an effective defence against artillery shells), and the characters alongside whom he served — the courageous private who transported wounded men to safety on a water-carrier donkey; the general who swam enthusiastically in the sea within range of a Turkish gun battery; and the soldier whose preferred service uniform comprised 'only a hat, pants, boots and his smile' . . .

JOSEPH LIEVESLEY BEESTON

◆

FIVE MONTHS AT ANZAC

A Narrative of Personal Experiences
of the Officer Commanding the
4th Field Ambulance,
Australian Imperial Force

Complete and Unabridged

ULVERSCROFT
Leicester

First published in Australia in 1916

This Large Print Edition
published 2016

A catalogue record for this book is available
from the British Library.

ISBN 978–1–4448–2686–9

Published by
F. A. Thorpe (Publishing)
Anstey, Leicestershire

Set by Words & Graphics Ltd.
Anstey, Leicestershire
Printed and bound in Great Britain by
T. J. International Ltd., Padstow, Cornwall

This book is printed on acid-free paper

SPECIAL MESSAGE TO READERS

THE ULVERSCROFT FOUNDATION
(registered UK charity number 264873)
was established in 1972 to provide funds for
resea   s.

- The Chuac   at   elc Eye
  Hospital, London
- The Ulverscroft Children's Eye Unit at Great
  Ormond Street Hospital for Sick Children
- Funding research into eye diseases and
  treatment at the Department of Ophthalmology,
  University of Leicester
- The Ulverscroft Vision Research Group,
  Institute of Child Health
- Twin operating theatres at the Western
  Ophthalmic Hospital, London
- The Chair of Ophthalmology at the Royal
  Australian College of Ophthalmologists

You can help further the work of the Foundation
by making a donation or leaving a legacy.
Every contribution is gratefully received. If you
would like to help support the Foundation or
require further information, please contact:

THE ULVERSCROFT FOUNDATION
The Green, Bradgate Road, Anstey
Leicester LE7 7FU, England
Tel: (0116) 236 4325

website: www.foundation.ulverscroft.com

Joseph Lievesley Beeston was born in Newcastle, Australia in 1859. After receiving his early education in the same city, he travelled to Ireland to take his medical degrees, returning to Australia to become assistant to his former mentor Dr. Knaggs. During the First World War, Lieutenant-Colonel Beeston, commanding the Fourth Field Ambulance, served with distinction on the Gallipoli Peninsula, receiving a field promotion to Colonel. Invalided back to England, he was decorated by King George at Buckingham Palace with the CMG, in addition to receiving the VD award for long service. Back in Australia, he resumed his professional duties, also participating in Parliamentary and civic affairs, and holding a number of honorary positions at Newcastle Hospital. Beeston died in 1921 from sudden heart failure, leaving a widow and three children, and was buried with full military honours. Well-liked and respected by his friends, colleagues and the community, his obituary spoke warmly of his kindly nature and generous disposition.

DEDICATED TO

THE OFFICERS, NON-COMMISSIONED
OFFICERS AND MEN OF THE 4th FIELD
AMBULANCE, A.I.F.,
OF WHOSE LOYALTY AND DEVOTION TO
DUTY THE WRITER HEREBY EXPRESSES
HIS DEEP APPRECIATION.

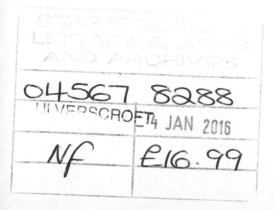

Contents

1

Fourth Field Ambulance

Shortly after the outbreak of War — after the first contingent had been mobilised, and while they were undergoing training — it became evident that it would be necessary to raise another force to proceed on the heels of the first. Three Infantry Brigades with their Ambulances had already been formed; orders for a fourth were now issued, and naturally the Ambulance would be designated Fourth Field Ambulance.

The Fourth Brigade was composed of the 13th Battalion (N.S.W.), 14th (Victoria), 15th (Queensland) and 16th (Western Australia) — commanded respectively by Lieutenant-Colonel Burnage, Lieutenant-Colonel Courtnay, Lieutenant-Colonel Cannon and Lieutenant-Colonel Pope. The Brigade was in charge of Colonel Monash, V.D., with Lieutenant-Colonel McGlinn as his Brigade Major.

As it will be necessary from time to time to allude to the component parts of the Ambulance, it may be as well to describe how an ambulance is made up. It is composed of

1

three sections, known as A, B, and C, the total of all ranks being 254 on a war strength. It is subdivided into Bearer, Tent and Transport Divisions. Each section has its own officers, and is capable of acting independently. Where there is an extended front, it is frequently desirable to detach sections and send them to positions where the work is heaviest.

★   ★   ★

As the name implies, the Bearers convey the wounded to the dressing station (or Field Hospital, as the case may be). Those in the Tent Division dress the cases and perform nursing duties, while the Transport Division undertakes their conveyance to Base Hospital.

It was decided to recruit the Fourth Field Ambulance from three States, A Section from Victoria, B from South Australia, C from Western Australia. Recruiting started in Broadmeadows, Victoria, on the 19th October, 1914, and thirty men enrolled from New South Wales were included in A Section. Towards the end of November B Section from South Australia joined us, and participated in the training. On the 22nd December we embarked on a transport forming one of a convoy of eighteen ships. The nineteenth ship

— joined after we left Albany.

Details from the Ambulance were supplied to different ships and the officers distributed among the fleet. Our last port in Australia was Albany, which was cleared on the last day of 1914 — a beautiful night and clear day, with the sea as smooth as the proverbial glass.

2

The Voyage

The convoy was under the command of Captain Brewis — a most capable and courteous officer, but a strict disciplinarian. To a landsman, his control of the various ships and his forethought in obtaining supplies seemed little short of marvellous. I had the good fortune to be associated with Captain Brewis on the passage from Colombo to Alexandria on board the — and his friendship is a pleasant memory.

The fleet was arranged in three lines, each ship being about three lengths astern of the one ahead. The sight was most inspiriting, and made one feel proud of the privilege of participation. The — towed the submarine AE2, and kept clear of the convoy, sometimes ahead, then astern, so that we viewed the convoy from all points.

The day after leaving Albany a steamer, which proved to be the — , joined us with C Section of our Ambulance. Signals were made for the — to move ahead and the — to drop astern, the — moving into the vacant place.

The manoeuvre was carried out in a most seamanlike manner, and Captain Young of the — received many compliments on his performance.

Three days later a message was flagged from the — that Major Stewart (who commanded the C Section of the Ambulance) was ill with enteric, and that his condition was serious. The flagship then sent orders (also by flag): 'Colonel Beeston will proceed to — and will remain there until next port. — to provide transport.' A boat was hoisted out, and Sergeant Draper as a nurse, Walkley my orderly, my little dog Paddy and I were lowered from the boat deck. What appeared smooth water proved to a long undulating swell; no water was shipped, but the fleet at times was not visible when the boat was in the trough of the sea.

However, the — was manoeuvred so as to form a shelter, and we gained the deck by means of the companion ladder as comfortably as if we had been in harbour. Major Stewart's illness proved to be of such a nature that his disembarkation at Colombo was imperative, and on our arrival there he was left in the hospital.

The heat in the tropics was very oppressive, and the horses suffered considerably. One day all the ships carrying horses were turned about and steamed for twenty minutes in the opposite direction in order to obtain a breath of air for the poor animals. In the holds the temperature was 90° and steamy at that. The sight of horses down a ship's hold is a novel one. Each is in a stall of such dimensions that the animal cannot be knocked about. All heads are inwards, and each horse has his own trough. At a certain time in the day lucerne hay is issued. This is the signal for a prodigious amount of stamping and noise on the part of the animals. They throw their heads about, snort and neigh, and seem as if they would jump over the barriers in their frantic effort to get a good feed. Horses on land are nice beasts, but on board ship they are a totally different proposition. One intelligent neddy stabled just outside my cabin spent the night in stamping on an adjacent steam pipe; consequently my sleep was of a disturbed nature, and not so restful as one might look for on a sea voyage. When he became tired, the brute on the opposite side took up the refrain, so that it seemed like Morse signalling on a large scale.

We reached Colombo on the 13th January, and found a number of ships of various nationalities in the harbour. Our convoy almost filled it. We were soon surrounded by boats offering for sale all sorts of things, mostly edibles. Of course no one was allowed on board.

After arranging for Major Stewart's accommodation at the hospital, we transferred from the — to the — . The voyage was resumed on the 15th. When a few days out, one of the ships flagged that there were two cases of appendicitis on board. The convoy was stopped; the ship drew near ours, and lowered a boat with the two cases, which was soon alongside. Meanwhile a large box which had been made by our carpenter was lowered over the side by a winch on the boat deck; the cases were placed in it and hoisted aboard, where the stretcher-bearers conveyed them to the hospital. Examination showed that operation was necessary in both cases, and the necessary preparations were made.

The day was a glorious one — not a cloud in the sky, and the sea almost oily in its smoothness. As the hospital was full of cases of measles, it was decided to operate on deck a little aft of the hospital. A guard was placed to keep inquisitive onlookers at a distance, and the two operations were carried out successfully. It was a novel experience to operate under these conditions. When one looked up from the work, instead of the usual tiled walls of a hospital theatre, one saw nothing but the sea and the transports. After all, they were ideal conditions; for the air was absolutely pure and free from any kind of germ.

While the convoy was stopped, the opportunity was taken to transfer Lieutenant-Colonel Bean from the — to the — . There had been a number of fatal cases on board the latter vessel, and it was deemed advisable to place a senior officer on board.

On arrival at Aden I had personal experience of the worth of the Red Cross Society. A number of cases had died aboard one of the transports, and I had to go over to investigate. The sea was fairly rough, the boat rising and falling ten or twelve feet. For a landsman to gain a ladder on a ship's side under these conditions is not a thing of undiluted joy. Anyhow I missed the ladder and went into the water. The first fear one had was that the boat would drop on one's head; however, I was hauled on board by two hefty sailors. The inspection finished, we were rowed back to our own ship, wet and cold. By the time 'home' was reached I felt pretty chilly; a hot bath soon put me right, and a dressing gown was dug out of the Red Cross goods supplied to the ship, in which I remained while my clothes were drying. Sewn inside was a card on which was printed: 'Will the recipient kindly write his personal experiences to George W. Parker, Daylesford, Victoria, Australia.' I wrote to Mr. Parker from Suez. I would recommend everyone sending articles of this kind to put a similar notice inside. To be able to acknowledge kindness is as gratifying to the recipient as the knowledge of its usefulness is to the giver.

The voyage to Suez (which was reached on the 28th January) was uneventful. We arrived there about 4 in the morning and found most of our convoy around us when we got on deck at daylight. Here we got news of the Turks' attack on the Canal. We heard that there had been a brush with the Turks, in which Australians had participated, and all the ships were to be sandbagged round the bridge. Bags of flour were used on the — .

The submarine cast off from the — outside and came alongside our ship. I was invited to go and inspect her, and Paddy accompanied me. On going below, however, I left him on the deck, and by some means he slipped overboard (this appears to run in the family on this trip); one of the crew fished him out, and he was sent up on to the — . When I got back I found Colonel Monash, the Brigadier, running up and down the deck with the dog so that he would not catch cold! The Colonel was almost as fond of the dog as I was.

9

3

Egypt

All along the canal we saw troops entrenched — chiefly Indians. This at the time was very novel — we little knew then how familiar trenches would become. At various points — about every four or five miles — a warship was passed. The troops on each ship stood to attention and the bugler blew the general salute. Port Said was reached in the afternoon, and here a great calamity overtook me. Paddy was lost! He was seen going ashore in the boat which took the mails. Though orders were out against anyone's leaving the ship, Colonel Monash offered me permission to go and look for him. With Sergeant Nickson and Walkley I started off and tramped through all sorts of slums and places, without any success. Finally we returned to the water front, where one of the natives (a little more intelligent than the others) took me to the Custom House close by. One of the officials could speak a little English, and in response to my enquiry he turned up a large book. Then I saw, among a

10

lot of Egyptian writing, PADDY 4 A.M.C. MORMON. This corresponded to his identity disc, which was round his neck. He was out at the abattoirs, where after a three-mile drive we obtained him. His return to the ship was hailed by the men with vociferous cheers.

On arrival at Alexandria we made arrangements for the disembarkation of all our sick, Lieutenant-Colonel Beach superintending their transport. We left soon after by rail for Heilwan, arriving after nightfall. A guide was detailed to conduct us to camp, and we set out to march a couple of miles across the desert. It was quite cold, so that the march was rather good; but, loaded as we were, in full marching order and soft after a long sea voyage, it was a stiff tramp. In the pitch dark, as silent as the grave, we stumbled along, and finally arrived at the camp outside Heliopolis, a place known as the Aerodrome.

Lieutenant-Colonel Sutherland and Major Helsham were camped with their Ambulance close by, and with most kindly forethought had pitched our tents for us. We just lay down in our greatcoats and slept until morning. Our Brigade was camped just across the road, and formed part of the New Zealand and Australian Division under General Sir Alexander Godley.

Training soon began, and everyone seemed

full of the idea of making himself 'fit'. Our peace camps and continuous training at home look very puny and small in comparison with the work which now occupied our time. At manoeuvres the number of troops might be anything up to thirty thousand. To march in the rear of such a column meant that each of the Ambulances soon swallowed its peck of dirt. But with it all we were healthy and vigorous. As an Ambulance we practiced all sorts of movements. Under supposition that we might have to retreat suddenly, the whole camp would be struck, packed on the waggon and taken down the Suez road, where it was pitched again, ready to receive patients; then tents would be struck and a return made to camp. Or we would make a start after nightfall and practise the movements without lights; the transport handling the horses in the dark. Or the different sections would march out independently, and concentrate on a point agreed upon. It was great practice, but in the end not necessary; for we went, not to France, as we expected, but to Gallipoli, where we had no horses. However, it taught the men to believe in themselves. That period of training was great. Everyone benefited, and by the beginning of April we felt fit for anything.

We were exceedingly well looked after in

the way of a standing camp. Sand of course was everywhere, but when watered it became quite hard, and the quadrangle made a fine drill ground. Each unit had a mess house in which the men had their meals; there was an abundant supply of water obtained from the Nile, so that shower baths were plentiful. Canteens were established, and the men were able to supplement their rations. The Y.M.C.A. erected buildings for the men's entertainment, which served an excellent purpose in keeping the troops in camp. Cinematographs showed pictures, and all round the camp dealers established shops, so that there was very little inducement for men to leave at night. A good deal of our time was occupied in weeding out undesirables from the Brigade. Thank goodness, I had not to send a man from the Ambulance back for this reason.

Apart from the instructive side of our stay in Egypt, the sojourn was most educational. We were camped just on the edge of the Land of Goshen; the place where Joseph obtained his wife was only about a mile away from my tent, and the well where the Virgin Mother rested with our Saviour was in close proximity. The same water wheels are here as are mentioned in the Bible, and one can see the camels and asses brought to water, and the women going to and fro with pitchers on their heads. Then in the museum in Cairo one could see the mummy of the Pharaoh of Joseph's time. All this made the Bible quite the most interesting book to read.

The troops having undergone pretty strenuous training, we were inspected by Sir Ian Hamilton, who was to command us in the forthcoming campaign. Then, early in April, the commanding officers of units were assembled at Headquarters and the different ships allotted. Finally, on the evening of the 11th April, our camp was struck, and we bade good-bye to Heliopolis. The waggons were packed and the Ambulance moved off, marching to the Railway Station in Cairo. Nine-thirty was the time fixed for our entraining, and we were there on the minute — and it was as well that such was the case, for General Williams stood at the gate to watch proceedings.

The waggons with four horses (drivers mounted, of course) were taken at a trot up an incline, through a narrow gateway on to the platform. The horses were then taken out and to the rear, and the waggons placed on the trucks by Egyptian porters.

We had 16 vehicles, 69 horses, 10 officers and 245 men. The whole were entrained in 35 minutes. The General was very pleased with the performance, and asked me to convey his approbation to the men. Certainly they did well.

4

To Gallipoli

At midnight we left Cairo and arrived at daybreak at Alexandria, the train running right on to the wharf, alongside which was the transport to convey us to Gallipoli — the Dardanelles we called it then. Loading started almost immediately, and I found that I — who in ordinary life am a peaceful citizen and a surgeon by profession — had to direct operations by which our waggons were to be removed from the railway trucks on to the wharf and thence to the ship's hold. Men with some knowledge of the mysteries of steam winches had to be specially selected and instructed in these duties, and I — well, beyond at times watching a ship being loaded at Newcastle, I was as innocent of their details as the unborn babe. However, everyone went at it, and the transport was loaded soon after dinner. We had the New Zealand Battery of Artillery, Battery Ammunition Column, 14th Battalion Transport and Army Service Corps with us, the whole numbering 560 men and 480 horses. At

4 p.m. the ship cast off, and we went to the outer harbour and began to shake down. The same hour the next day saw us under weigh for the front. The voyage was quite uneventful, the sea beautifully calm, and the various islands in the Egean Sea most picturesque. Three days later we arrived at Lemnos, and found the harbour (which is of considerable size) packed with warships and transports. I counted 20 warships of various sizes and nationalities. The *Agamemnon* was just opposite us, showing signs of the damage she had received in the bombardment of the Turkish forts a couple of months before. We stayed here a week, and every day practised going ashore in boats, each man in full marching order leaving the ship by the pilot ladder.

It is extraordinary how one adapts oneself to circumstances. For years it has been almost painful to me to look down from a height; as for going down a ladder, in ordinary times I could not do it. However, here there was no help for it; a commanding officer cannot order his men to do what he will not do himself, so up and down we went in full marching order. Bearer work was carried out among the stony hills which surround the harbour.

Finally, on the 24th April, the whole armada got under weigh, headed by the

Queen Elizabeth, or as the men affectionately termed her, 'Lizzie'. We had been under steam for only about four hours when a case of smallpox was reported on board. As the captain informed me he had time to spare, we returned to Lemnor and landed the man, afterwards proceeding on our journey. At night the ship was darkened. Our ship carried eight horse-boats, which were to be used by the 29th Division in their landing at Cape Helles.

Just about dawn on Sunday the 25th I came on deck and could see the forms of a number of warships in close proximity to us, with destroyers here and there and numbers of transports. Suddenly one ship fired a gun, and then they were all at it, the Turks replying in quick time from the forts on Seddul Bahr, as well as from those on the Asiatic side. None of our ships appeared to be hit, but great clouds of dust were thrown up in the forts opposite us. Meanwhile destroyers were passing us loaded with troops, and barges filled with grim and determined-looking men were being towed towards the shore. One could not help wondering how many of them would be alive in an hour's time. Slowly they neared the cliffs; as the first barge appeared to ground, a burst of fire broke out along the beach, alternately rifles and machine guns.

The men leaped out of the barges — almost at once the firing on the beach ceased, and more came from halfway up the cliff. The troops had obviously landed, and were driving the Turks back. After a couple of hours the top of the cliff was gained; there the troops became exposed to a very heavy fire from some batteries of artillery placed well in the rear, to which the warships attended as soon as they could locate them. The *Queen Elizabeth* was close by us, apparently watching a village just under the fort. Evidently some guns were placed there. She loosed off her two fifteen-inch guns, and after the dust had cleared away we could see that new streets had been made for the inhabitants. Meanwhile the British had gained the top and were making headway, but losing a lot of men — one could see them falling everywhere.

5

The Anzac Landing

The horse-boats having been got overboard, we continued our voyage towards what is now know as Anzac. Troops — Australians and New Zealanders — were being taken ashore in barges. Warships were firing apparently as fast as they could load, the Turks replying with equal cordiality. In fact, as Captain Dawson remarked to me, it was quite the most 'willing' Sunday he had ever seen.

Our troops were ascending the hills through a dwarf scrub, just low enough to let us see the men's heads, though sometimes we could only locate them by the glint of the bayonets in the sunshine. Everywhere they were pushing on in extended order, but many falling. The Turks appeared to have the range pretty accurately. About mid-day our men seemed to be held up, the Turkish shrapnel appearing to be too much for them. It was now that there occurred what I think one of the finest incidents of the campaign. This was the landing of the Australian Artillery. They got two of their guns ashore, and over very rough country dragged them up the hills with what looked like a hundred men to each. Up they went, through a wheat-field, covered and plastered with shrapnel, but with never a stop until the crest of the hill on the right was reached. Very little time was wasted in getting into action, and from this time it became evident that we were there to stay.

The practice of the naval guns was simply perfect. They lodged shell after shell just in front of the foremost rank of our men; in response to a message asking them to clear one of the gullies, one ship placed shell after shell up that gully, each about a hundred yards apart, and in as straight a line as if they were ploughing the ground for Johnny Turk, instead of making the place too hot to hold him.

The Turks now began to try for this warship, and in their endeavours almost succeeded in getting the vessel we were on, as a shell burst right overhead.

The wounded now began to come back, and the one hospital ship there was filled in a very short time. Every available transport was then utilised for the reception of casualties, and as each was filled she steamed off to the base at Alexandria. As night came on we appeared to have a good hold of the place, and orders came for our bearer division to land. They took with them three days' 'iron' rations, which consisted of a tin of bully beef, a bag of small biscuits, and some tea and sugar, dixies, a tent, medical comforts, and (for firewood) all the empty cases we could scrape up in the ship. Each squad had a set of splints, and every man carried a tourniquet and two roller bandages in his pouch. Orders were issued that the men were to make the contents of their water-bottles last three days, as no water was available on shore.

The following evening the remainder of the Ambulance, less the transport, was ordered ashore. We embarked in a trawler, and steamed towards the shore in the growing dusk as far as the depth of water would allow. The night was bitterly cold, it was raining, and all felt this was real soldiering. None of us could understand what occasioned the noise we heard at times, of something hitting the iron deck houses behind us; at last one of the men exclaimed: 'Those are bullets, sir,' so that we were having our baptism of fire. It was marvellous that no one was hit, for they were fairly frequent, and we all stood closely packed. Finally the skipper of the trawler, Captain Hubbard, told me he did not think we could be taken off that night, and therefore intended to drop anchor. He invited Major Meikle and myself to the cabin, where the cook served out hot tea to all hands. I have drunk a considerable number of cups of tea in my time, but that mug was very, very nice. The night was spent dozing where we stood, Paddy being very disturbed with the noise of the guns.

At daylight a barge was towed out and, after placing all our equipment on board, we started for the beach. As soon as the barge grounded, we jumped out into the water (which was about waist deep) and got to dry land. Colonel Manders, the A.D.M.S. of our Division, was there, and directed us up a gully where we were to stay in reserve for the time being, meantime to take lightly-wounded cases. One tent was pitched and dug-outs made for both men and patients, the Turks supplying shrapnel pretty freely. Our position happened to be in rear of a mountain battery, whose guns the Turks appeared very anxious to silence, and any shells the battery did not want came over to us. As soon as we were settled down I had time to look round. Down on the beach the 1st Casualty Clearing Station (under Lieutenant-Colonel Giblin) and the Ambulance of the Royal Marine Light Infantry were at work. There were scores of casualties awaiting treatment, some of them horribly knocked about. It was my first experience of such a number of cases. In civil practice, if an accident took place in which three or four men were injured, the occurrence would be deemed out of the ordinary: but here there were almost as many hundreds, and all the flower of Australia. It made one feel really that, in the words of General Sherman, 'War is hell', and it seemed damnable that it should be in the power of one man, even if be he the German Emperor, to decree that all these men should be mutilated or killed. The great majority were just coming into manhood with all their life before them. The stoicism and fortitude with which they bore their pain was truly remarkable. Every one of them was cheery and optimistic; there was not a murmur; the only requests were for a cigarette or a drink of water. One felt very proud of these Australians, each waiting his turn to be dressed without complaining. It really quite unnerved me for a time. However, it was no time to allow the sentimental side of one's nature to come uppermost.

I watched the pinnaces towing the barges in. Each pinnace belonged to a warship and was in charge of a midshipman — dubbed by his shipmates a 'snotty'. This name originates from the days of Trafalgar. The little chaps appear to have suffered from chronic colds in the head, with the usual accompaniment of a copious flow from the nasal organs. Before addressing an officer the boys would clean their faces by drawing the sleeve of their jacket across the nose; and, I understand that this practice so incensed Lord Nelson that he ordered three brass buttons to be sewn on the wristbands of the boys' jackets. However, this is by the way. These boys, of all ages from 14 to 16, were steering their pinnaces with supreme indifference to the shrapnel falling about, disdaining any cover and as cool as if there was no such thing as war. I spoke to one, remarking that they were having a great time. He was a bright, chubby, sunny-faced little chap, and with a smile said: 'Isn't it beautiful, sir? When we started, there were sixteen of us, and now there are only six!' This is the class of man they make officers out of in Britain's navy, and while this is so there need be no fear of the result of any encounter with the Germans.

Another boy, bringing a barge full of men ashore, directed them to lie down and take all the cover they could, he meanwhile steering the pinnace and standing quite unconcernedly with one foot on the boat's rail.

6

At Work on the Peninsula

Casualties began to come in pretty freely, so that our tent was soon filled. We now commenced making dug-outs in the side of the gully and placing the men in these. Meantime stores of all kinds were being accumulated on the beach — stacks of biscuits, cheese and preserved beef, all of the best. One particular kind of biscuit, known as the 'forty-niners', had forty-nine holes in it, was believed to take forty-nine years to bake, and needed forty-nine chews to a bite. But there were also beautiful hams and preserved vegetables, and with these and a tube of Oxo a very palatable soup could be prepared. A well-known firm in England puts up a tin which they term an Army Ration, consisting of meat and vegetables, nicely seasoned and very palatable. For a time this ration was eagerly looked for and appreciated, but later on, when the men began to get stale, it did not agree with them so well; it appeared to be too rich for many of us. We had plenty of jam, of a kind — one kind. Oh! how we used to revile the maker of 'Damson and Apple'! The damson coloured it, and whatever they used for apple gave it body.

One thing was good all the time, and that was the tea. The brand never wavered, and the flavour was always full. Maynard could always make a good cup of it. It has been already mentioned that water was not at first available on shore. This was soon overcome, thanks to the Navy. They convoyed water barges from somewhere, which they placed along shore; the water was then pumped into our water carts, and the men filled their water-bottles from them. The water, however, never appeared to quench our thirst. It was always better made up into tea, or taken with lime juice when we could get it.

Tobacco, cigarettes and matches were on issue, but the tobacco was of too light a brand for me, so that Walkley used to trade off my share of the pernicious weed for matches. The latter became a precious commodity. I have seen three men light their pipes from one match. Captain Welch was very independent; he had a burning glass, and obtained his light from the sun. After a few days the R.M.L.I. were ordered away, and we were directed to take up their position on the beach. A place for operating was prepared by putting sandbags at either end, the roof being formed by planks covered with sandbags and loose earth. Stanchions of 4×4 in. timber were driven into the ground, with crosspieces at a convenient height; the stretcher was placed on these, and thus an operating table was formed. Shelves were made to hold our instruments, trays and bottles; these were all in charge of Staff-Sergeant Henderson, a most capable and willing assistant. Close by a kitchen was made, and a cook kept constantly employed keeping a supply of hot water, bovril, milk and biscuits ready for the men when they came in wounded, for they had to be fed as well as medically attended to.

7

Incidents and Yarns

One never ceased admiring our men, and their cheeriness under these circumstances and their droll remarks caused us many a laugh. One man, just blown up by a shell, informed us that it was a — of a place — 'no place to take a lady'. Another told of the mishap to his 'cobber', who picked up a bomb and blew on it to make it light: 'All at once it blew his — head off — Gorblime! you would have laughed!' For lurid and perfervid language commend me to the Australian Tommy. Profanity oozes from him like music from a barrel organ. At the same time, he will give you his idea of the situation, almost without exception in an optimistic strain, generally concluding his observation with the intimation that 'We gave them hell'. I have seen scores of them lying wounded and yet chatting one to another while waiting their turn to be dressed. The stretcher-bearers were a fine body of men. Prior to this campaign, the Army Medical Corps was always looked upon as a soft job. In peacetime we had to submit to all sorts of flippant remarks, and were called Linseed Lancers, Body-snatchers, and other cheery and jovial names; but, thanks to Abdul and the cordiality of his reception, the A.A.M.C. can hold up their heads with any of the fighting troops. It was a common thing to hear men say: 'This beach is a hell of a place! The trenches are better than this.' The praises of the stretcher-bearers were in all the men's mouths; enough could not be said in their favour. Owing to the impossibility of landing the transport, all the wounded had to be carried; often for a distance of a mile and a half, in a blazing sun, and through shrapnel and machine-gun fire. But there was never a flinch; through it all they went, and performed their duty. Of our Ambulance 185 men and officers landed, and when I relinquished command, 43 remained. At one time we were losing so many bearers, that carrying during the day-time was abandoned, and orders were given that it should only be undertaken after night-fall. On one occasion a man was being sent off to the hospital ship from our tent in the gully. He was not very bad, but he felt like being carried down. As the party went along the beach, Beachy Bill became active; one of the bearers lost his leg, the other was wounded, but the man who was being carried down got

30

up and ran! All the remarks I have made regarding the intrepidity and valour of the stretcher-bearers apply also to the regimental bearers. These are made up from the bandsmen. Very few people think, when they see the band leading the battalion in parade through the streets, what happens to them on active service. Here bands are not thought of; the instruments are left at the base, and the men become bearers, and carry the wounded out of the front line for the Ambulance men to care for. Many a stretcher-bearer has deserved the V.C.

One of ours told me they had reached a man severely wounded in the leg, in close proximity to his dug-out. After he had been placed on the stretcher and made comfortable, he was asked whether there was anything he would like to take with him. He pondered a bit, and then said: 'Oh! you might give me my diary — I would like to make a note of this before I forget it!'

It can be readily understood that in dealing with large bodies of men, such as ours, a considerable degree of organization is necessary, in order to keep an account, not only of the man, but of the nature of his injury (or illness, as the case may be) and of his destination. Without method chaos would soon reign. As each casualty came in he was examined, and dressed or operated upon as the necessity arose. Sergeant Baxter then got orders from the officer as to where the case was to be sent. A ticket was made out, containing the man's name, his regimental number, the nature of his complaint, whether morphia had been administered and the quantity, and finally his destination. All this was also recorded in our books, and returns made weekly, both to headquarters and to the base. Cases likely to recover in a fortnight's time were sent by fleet-sweeper to Mudros; the others were embarked on the hospital ship. They were placed in barges, and towed out by a pinnace to a trawler, and by that to the hospital ship, where the cases were sorted out. When once they had left the beach, our knowledge of them ceased, and of course our responsibility. One man arriving at the hospital ship was describing, with the usual picturesque invective, how the bullet had got into his shoulder. One of the officers, who apparently was unacquainted with the Australian vocabulary, said: 'What was that you said, my man?' The reply came, 'A blightah ovah theah put a bullet in heah.'

At a later period a new gun had come into action on our left, which the men christened 'Windy Annie'. Beachy Bill occupied the olive grove, and was on our right. Annie was getting the range of our dressing station pretty accurately, and requisition on the Engineers evoked the information that sandbags were not available. However, the Army Service came to our rescue with some old friends, the 'forty-niners'. Three tiers of these in their boxes defied the shells just as they defied our teeth.

As the sickness began to be more manifest, it became necessary to enlarge the accommodation in our gully. The hill was dug out, and the soil placed in bags with which a wall was built, the intervening portion being filled up with the remainder of the hill. By this means we were able to pitch a second tent and house more of those who were slightly ill. It was in connection with this engineering scheme that I found the value of W.O. Cosgrove. He was possessed of a good deal of the *suaviter in modo*, and it was owing to his dextrous handling of Ordnance that we got such a fine supply of bags. This necessitated a redistribution of dug-outs, and a line of them was constructed sufficient to take a section of bearers. The men christened this 'Shrapnel Avenue'. They called my dug-out 'The Nut', because it held the 'Kernel'. I offer this with every apology. It's not my joke.

The new dug-outs were not too safe. Murphy was killed there one afternoon, and Claude Grime badly wounded later on.

Claude caused a good deal of amusement. He had a rooted objection to putting on clothes and wore only a hat, pants, boots and his smile. Consequently his body became quite mahogany-coloured. When he was wounded he was put under an anaesthetic so that I could search for the bullet. As the anaesthetic began to take effect, Claude talked the usual unintelligible gibberish. Now, we happened to have a Turkish prisoner at the time, and in the midst of Claude's struggles and shouts in rushed an interpreter. He looked round, and promptly came over to Claude, uttering words which I suppose were calculated to soothe a wounded Turk; and we had some difficulty in assuring him that the other man, not Claude, was the Turk he was in quest of.

8

Air Fighting

The German aeroplanes flew over our gully pretty regularly. As first we were rather perturbed, as they had a nasty habit of dropping bombs, but as far as I know they never did any damage. Almost all the bombs dropped into the water. One of them sent some steel arrows down, about six or eight inches in length, with a metal point something like a carpenter's bit. In order to conceal our tents, we covered them with holly-bushes, cut and placed over the canvas. Our aeroplanes were constantly up, and were easily recognised by a red ring painted underneath, while the Taube was adorned with a large black cross; but after we had been there a little time we found it was not necessary to use glasses in order to ascertain whose flying machine was over us; we were able to tell by listening, as their engines had a different sound from those belonging to us.

Our aeroplanes were the source of a good deal of annoyance to the Turks. They continually fired at them, but, as far as I was able to judge, never went within cooee of one. The bursts of shrapnel away in the air made a pretty sight, puffs of white smoke like bits of cotton-wool in succession, and the aeroplane sailing unconcernedly along. It appears to be very difficult to judge distance away in the air, and even more difficult to estimate the rate at which the object is travelling. What became of the shell-cases of the shrapnel used to puzzle us. One day Walkley remarked that it was peculiar that none fell on us. I replied, 'Surely there is plenty of room other than where we are for them to fall.' Scarcely were the words uttered than down one came close by. We knew it was a case from above and not one fired direct, because the noise was so different.

The hydroplanes used by the Navy were interesting. Floating on the water, they would gather way and soar upwards like a bird. Their construction was different from that of the aeroplanes.

A captive balloon was used a good deal to give the ranges for the warships. It was carried on the forepart of a steamer and was, I believe, in connection with it by telephone or wireless.

9

The Officers' Mess

We kept up the custom of having an officers' mess right through the campaign. When we first landed, while everything was in confusion, each man catered for himself; but it was a lonely business, and not conducive to health. When a man cooked his own rations he probably did not eat much. So a dug-out was made close to the hospital tent, and we all had our meals together. A rather pathetic incident occurred one day. Just after we had finished lunch three of us were seated, talking of the meals the 'Australia' provided, when a fragment of shell came through the roof on to the table and broke one of the enamel plates. This may seem a trivial affair and not worth grousing about; but the sorry part of it was that we only had one plate each, and this loss entailed one man having to wait until the others had finished their banquet.

I have elsewhere alluded to the stacks of food on the beach. Amongst them bully beef was largely in evidence. Ford, our cook, was very good in always endeavouring to disguise the fact that 'Bully' was up again. He used to fry it; occasionally he got curry powder from the Indians and persuaded us that the resultant compound was curried goose; but it was bully beef all the time. Then he made what he called rissoles — onions entered largely into their framework, and when you opened them you wanted to get out into the fresh air. Preserved potatoes, too, were very handy. We had them with our meat, and what remained over we put treacle on, and ate as pancakes. Walkley and Betts obtained flour on several occasions, and made very presentable pancakes. John Harris, too, was a great forager — he knew exactly where to put his hand on decent biscuits, and the smile with which he landed his booty made the goods toothsome in the extreme. Harris had a gruesome experience. One day he was seated on a hill, talking to a friend, when a shell took the friend's head off and scattered his brains over Harris.

Before leaving the description of the officers' mess, I must not omit to introduce our constant companions, the flies. As Australians we rather prided ourselves on our judgment regarding these pests, and in Gallipoli we had every opportunity of putting our faculties to the test. There were flies, big horse flies, blue flies, green flies, and flies.

They turned up everywhere and with everything. While one was eating one's food with the right hand, one had to keep the left going with a wisp, and even then the flies beat us. Then we always had the comforting reflection of those dead Turks not far away — the distance being nothing to a fly. In order to get a little peace at one meal in the day, our dinner hour was put back until dusk. Men wounded had a horrible time. Fortunately we had a good supply of mosquito netting purchased with the Red Cross money. It was cut up into large squares and each bearer had a supply.

10

The Armistice

On the 23rd of May anyone looking down the coast could see a man on Gaba Tepe waving a white flag. He was soon joined by another occupied in a like manner. Some officers came into the Ambulance and asked for the loan of some towels; we gave them two, which were pinned together with safety pins. White flags don't form part of the equipment of Australia's army.

Seven mounted men had been observed coming down Gaba Tepe, and they were joined on the beach by our four. The upshot was that one was brought in blindfolded to General Birdwood. Shortly after we heard it announced that a truce had been arranged for the following day in order to bury the dead.

The following morning Major Millard and I started from our right and walked up and across the battle-field. It was a stretch of country between our lines and those of the Turks, and was designated No Man's Land. At the extreme right there was a small farm; the owner's house occupied part of it, and was just as the man had left it. Our guns had knocked it about a good deal. In close proximity was a field of wheat, in which there were scores of dead Turks. As these had been dead anything from a fortnight to three weeks their condition may be better imagined than described. One body I saw was lying with the leg shattered. He had crawled into a depression in the ground and lay with his great-coat rolled up for a pillow; the stains on the ground showed that he had bled to death, and it can only be conjectured how long he lay there before death relieved him of his sufferings. Scores of the bodies were simply riddled with bullets. Midway between the trenches a line of Turkish sentries were posted. Each was in a natty blue uniform with gold braid, and top boots, and all were done 'up to the nines'. Each stood by a white flag on a pole stuck in the ground. We buried all the dead on our side of this line and they performed a similar office for those on their side. Stretchers were used to carry the bodies, which were all placed in large trenches. The stench was awful, and many of our men wore handkerchiefs over their mouths in their endeavour to escape it. I counted two thousand dead Turks. One I judged to be an officer of rank, for the bearers carried him shoulder-high down a gully to the rear. The ground was absolutely covered with rifles and equipment of all kinds, shell-cases and caps, and ammunition clips. The rifles were all collected and the bolts removed to prevent their being used again. Some of the Turks were lying right on our trenches, almost in some of them. The Turkish sentries were peaceable-looking men, stolid in type and of the peasant class mostly. We fraternised with them and gave them cigarettes and tobacco. Some Germans were there, but they viewed us with malignant eyes. When I talked to Colonel Pope about it afterwards he said the Germans were a mean lot of beggars: 'Why,' said he most indignantly, 'they came and had a look into my trenches.' I asked, 'What did you do?' He replied, 'Well, I had a look at theirs.'

11

Torpedoing of the Triumph

The day after the armistice, at fifteen minutes after noon, I was in my dug-out when one of the men exclaimed that something was wrong with the *Triumph*. I ran out and was in time to see the fall of the water sent up by the explosive. It was a beautifully calm day, and the ship was about a mile and a quarter from us; she had a decided list towards us, and it was evident that something was radically wrong. With glasses one could see the men lined up in two ranks as if on parade, without the least confusion. Then two destroyers went over and put their noses on each side of the big ship's bows; all hands from the *Triumph* marched aboard the destroyers. She was gradually heeling over, and all movables were slipping into the sea. One of the destroyers barked three or four shots at something which we took to be the submarine. In fifteen minutes the *Triumph* was keel up, the water spurting from her different vent pipes as it was expelled by the imprisoned air. She lay thus for seventeen minutes, gradually getting lower and lower in the water, when quietly her stern rose and she slipped underneath, not a ripple remaining to show where she had sunk. I have often read of the vortex caused by a ship sinking, but as far as I could see there was in this case not the slightest disturbance. It was pathetic to see this beautiful ship torpedoed and in thirty-two minutes at the bottom of the sea. I believe the only lives lost were those of men injured by the explosion. Meanwhile five destroyers came up from Helles at a terrific speed, the water curling from their bows; they and all the other destroyers circled round and round the bay, but the submarine lay low and got off. Her commander certainly did his job well.

12

The Destroyers

After the torpedoing of the *Triumph* here, and the *Majestic* in the Straits all the big ships left and went to Mudros, as there was no sense in leaving vessels costing over a million each to the mercy of submarines. This gave the destroyers the chance of their lives. Up to this they had not been allowed to speak, but now they took on much of the bombardment required. They were constantly nosing about, and the slightest movement on the part of the Turks brought forth a bang from one of their guns. If a Turk so much as winked he received a rebuke from the destroyer. The Naval men all appeared to have an unbounded admiration for the Australians as soldiers, and boats rarely came ashore without bringing some fresh bread or meat or other delicacy; their tobacco, too, was much sought after. It is made up from the leaf, and rolled up in spun yarn. The flavour is full, and after a pipe of it — well, you feel that you have had a smoke.

13

The Indian Regiments

We had a good many Indian regiments in the Army Corps. The mountain battery occupied a position on 'Pluggey's Plateau' in the early stage of the campaign, and they had a playful way of handing out the shrapnel to the Turks. It was placed in boiling water to soften the resin in which the bullets are held. By this means the bullets spread more readily, much to the joy of the sender and the discomfiture of Abdul. The Indians were always very solicitous about their wounded. When one came in to be attended to, he was always followed by two of his chums bearing, one a water bottle, the other some food, for their caste prohibits their taking anything directly from our hands. When medicine had to be administered, the man came in, knelt down, and opened his mouth, and the medicine was poured into him without the glass touching his lips. Food was given in the same way. I don't know how they got on when they were put on the ship. When one was killed, he was wrapped up in a sheet and his comrades carried him shoulder-high to their cemetery, for they had a place set apart for their own dead. They were constantly squatting on their haunches making a sort of pancake. I tasted one; but it was too fatty and I spat it out, much to the amusement of the Indians.

One of them saw the humorous side of life. He described to Mr. Henderson the different attitudes adopted towards Turkish shells by the British, Indian and Australian soldiers. 'British Tommy,' said he, 'Turk shell, Tommy says, 'Ah!'. Turk shell, Indian say, 'Oosh!'. Australian say, 'Where the hell did that come from?'.'

The Divisional Ammunition Column was composed of Sikhs, and they were a brave body of men. It was their job to get the ammunition to the front line, so that they were always fair targets for the Turks. The mules were hitched up in threes, one in rear of the other, each mule carrying two boxes of ammunition. The train might number any-thing from 15 to 20 mules. All went along at a trot, constantly under fire. When a mule was hit he was unhitched, the boxes of ammuni-tion were rolled off, and the train proceeded; nothing stopped them. It was the same if one of the men became a casualty; he was put on one side to await the stretcher-bearers — but almost always one of the other men appeared with a water bottle.

They were very adept in the management of mules. Frequently a block would occur while the mule train occupied a sap; the mules at times became fractious and manipulated their hind legs with the most marvellous precision — certainly they placed a good deal of weight in their arguments. But in the midst of it all, when one could see nothing but mules' heels, straps and ammunition boxes, the Indian drivers would talk to their charges and soothe them down. I don't know what they said, but presume it resembled the cooing, coaxing and persuasive tongue of our bullock-driver. The mules were all stalled in the next gully to ours, and one afternoon three or four of us were sitting admiring the sunset when a shell came over. It was different from that usually sent by Abdul, being seemingly formed of paper and black rag; someone suggested, too, that there was a good deal of faultiness in the powder. From subsequent inquiries we found that what we saw going over our dug-outs was Mule! A shell had burst right in one of them, and the resultant mass was what we had observed. The Ceylon Tea Planter's Corps was bivouacked just below us and were having tea at the time; their repast was mixed with mule.

Donkeys formed part of the population of

the Peninsula. I am referring here to the four-footed variety, though, of course, others were in evidence at times. The Neddies were docile little beasts, and did a great deal of transport work. When we moved out in August, orders were issued that all equipment was to be carried. I pointed out a drove of ten of these little animals, which appeared handy and without an owner, and suggested to the men that they would look well with our brand on. It took very little time to round them up, cut a cross in the hair on their backs and place a brassard round their ears. They were then our property. The other type of donkey generally indulged in what were known as Furfys or Beachograms. Furfy originated in Broadmeadows, Victoria; the second title was born in the Peninsula. The least breath of rumour ran from mouth to mouth in the most astonishing way. Talk about a Bush Telegraph! It is a tortoise in its movements compared with a Beachogram. The number of times that Achi Baba fell cannot be accurately stated but it was twice a day at the least. A man came in to be dressed on one occasion; suddenly some pretty smart rifle fire broke out on the right. 'Hell!' said the man, 'what's up?' 'Oh!' said Captain Dawson. 'There's a war on — didn't you hear about it?'

14

The Swimming

One thing that was really good in Anzac was the swimming. At first we used to dive off the barges; then the Engineers built Watson's pier, at the end of which the water was fifteen feet deep and as clear as crystal, so that one could see every pebble at the bottom. At times the water was very cold, but always invigorating. General Birdwood was an enthusiastic swimmer, but he always caused me a lot of anxiety. That pier was well covered by Beachy Bill, and one never knew when he might choose to give it his attention. This did not deter the General. He came down most regularly, sauntered out to the end, went through a lot of Sandow exercises and finally jumped in. He then swam out to a buoy moored about a quarter of a mile away. On his return he was most leisurely in drying himself. Had anything happened to him I don't know what the men would have done, for he was adored by everyone.

Swimming was popular with all hands. Early in the campaign we had a Turkish attack one morning; it was over by midday, and an hour later most of the men were in swimming. I think it not unlikely that some of the 'missing' men were due to this habit. They would come to the beach and leave their clothes and identity discs ashore, and sometimes they were killed in the water. In this case there was no possibility of ascertaining their names. It often struck me that this might account for some whose whereabouts were unknown.

While swimming, the opportunity was taken by a good many to soak their pants and shirts, inside which there was, very often, more than the owner himself. I saw one man fish his pants out; after examining the seams, he said to his pal: 'They're not dead yet.' His pal replied: 'Never mind, you gave them a — of a fright.' These insects were a great pest, and I would counsel friends sending parcels to the soldiers to include a tin of insecticide; it was invaluable when it could be obtained. I got a fright myself one night. A lot of things were doing the Melbourne Cup inside my blanket. The horrible thought suggested itself that I had got 'them' too, but a light revealed the presence of fleas. These were very large able-bodied animals and became our constant companions at nighttime; in fact, one could only get to sleep after dosing the blanket with insecticide.

My little dog Paddy enjoyed the swim almost as much as I did. He was a great favourite with everybody but the Provost-Martial. This official was a terror for red tape, and an order came out that dogs were to be destroyed. That meant that the Military Police were after Paddy. However, I went to General Birdwood, who was very handsome about it, and gave me permission to keep the little chap. Almost immediately after he was reprieved he ran down to the Provost-Martial's dug-out and barked at him. Paddy was very nearly human. One day we were down as usual when Beachy Bill got busy, and I had to leave the pier with only boots and a smile on. I took refuge behind my old friends the biscuits, and Paddy ran out to each shell, barking until it exploded. Finally one burst over him and a bullet perforated his abdomen. His squeals were piteous. He lived until the next day, but he got a soldier's burial.

15

Turkish Prisoners

We saw a good many Turkish prisoners at one time or another, and invariably fraternised with them. They were kept inside a barbed-wire enclosure with a guard over them; but there was no need to prevent their escape — they would not leave if they got the chance. On one occasion twelve of them were told to go some distance into the scrub and bring in some firewood. No one was sent with them, the idea being to encourage them to go to their lines and persuade some of the Turks to desert to us. But they were like the cat; they all came back — with the firewood.

I saw two of our men on one occasion bringing in a prisoner. They halted on the hill opposite us, and one of them went to headquarters to ascertain how the prisoner was to be disposed of. In a very short time he was surrounded by fourteen or fifteen of our soldiers, trying to carry on a conversation, and giving him cigarettes and in fact anything he would accept. An hour before they had been trying their best to shoot one another.

In one of the attacks on our left the Turks were badly beaten off and left a lot of their dead close up to our trenches. As it was not safe to get over and remove the bodies, a number of boat-hooks were obtained, and with them the bodies were pulled in to our trenches. One of the 'bodies' proved to be a live Turk who had been unable to get back to his line for fear of being shot by our men. He was blindfolded and sent down to the compound with the other prisoners.

The difficulty of obtaining sufficient exercise was very great at times. We only held a piece of territory under a square mile in extent, and none of it was free from shell or rifle-fire, so that our perambulations were carried on under difficulty. Major Meikle and I had our regular walk before breakfast. At first we went down the beach towards Gaba Tepe, and then sat for a while talking and trying to see what we could see; but a sniper apparently used to watch for us, for we were invariably saluted by the ping of a rifle in the distance and the dust of the bullet in close proximity to our feet. We concluded that, if we continued to walk in this direction someone would be getting hurt, so our walks were altered to the road round 'Pluggey's Plateau'. We were seated there one morning when our howitzer in the gully was fired, and we felt that the shell was not far from where we sat. We went down to the Battery, and I interrogated some of the gunners. 'How far off the top of that hill does that shell go?' said I. 'About a yard, sir,' replied the man; 'one time we hit it.' I asked him if it would be convenient for the battery to elevate a bit if we were sitting there again.

16

Post Office

The postal arrangements on the whole were good, considering the circumstances under which the mails were handled. It was always a matter of interest for all of us when we saw mail-bags in the barges, whether or no we were to participate in the good luck of receiving letters. And here I might make the suggestion to correspondents in Australia to send as many snap-shot photos as possible. They tell more than a letter, for one can see how the loved ones are looking. Papers were what we needed most, and we got very few indeed of these. I wrote home once that I was fortunate in having a paper to read that had been wrapped round greasy bacon. This was a positive fact. We were up the gully at the advance dressing station, and a machine gun was playing right down the position. Four men were killed and six wounded right in front of us, so that it was not prudent to leave until night fell. It was then that reading matter became so necessary. The paper was the *Sydney Morning Herald* and contained an advertisement stating that there was a vacancy for two boarders at Katoomba; I was an applicant for the vacancy. The *Bulletin* was a God-send when it arrived, as was *Punch*. Norman Morris occasionally got files of the *Newcastle Morning Herald*, which he would hand on to us, as there were a lot of men from the Newcastle district in the Ambulance. Later on it was possible to register a small parcel in the Field Post Office — for home.

17

Sanitary Arrangements

In order to keep the health of the troops good it was necessary to be exceedingly careful in the matter of sanitation. Lieutenant-Colonel Millard was the Sanitary Officer for our Division, and Lieutenant-Colonel Stokes for the 1st Australian Division.

The garbage at first was collected in casks, placed in a barge and conveyed out into the bay; it was found, however, that a lot of it drifted back. It reminded one so much of Newcastle and Stockton. The same complaints were made by the men on the right as are put forth by Stockton residents regarding the Newcastle garbage. We, of course, occupied the position of the Newcastle Council, and were just as vehement in our denial of what was a most obvious fact. The situation was exactly the same — only that, instead of dead horses, there were dead mules. Three incinerators were started, enclosures built up with stone, and a fire lighted. This was effective, but gave rise to a very unpleasant smell along the beach. The only time I was shot was from an incinerator; a cartridge had been included in the rubbish and exploded just as I was passing. The bullet gave me a nasty knock on the shin.

It was a fairly common practice among men just arrived to put a cartridge in their fire just to hear the noise. Of course down on the beach it was not usual to hear a rifle fired at close range, and the sound would make everybody look up to see 'where the — that came from'. The discovery of the culprit would bring out a chorus from the working parties: 'Give him a popgun, give him a popgun!' 'Popgun' was preceded by the usual Australian expletive.

The water found on the Peninsula was always subjected to careful examination, and, before the troops were allowed to use it notices were placed on each well stating whether the water was to be boiled or if only to be used for washing.

18

Simpson

Everyone knows of Simpson and his donkey. This man belonged to one of the other Ambulances, but he made quite frequent trips backwards and forwards to the trenches, the donkey always carrying a wounded man. Simpson was frequently warned of the danger he ran, for he never stopped, no matter how heavy the firing was. His invariable reply was, 'My troubles!' The brave chap was killed in the end. His donkey was afterwards taken over by Johnstone, one of our men, who improvised stirrups out of the stretcher-slings, and conveyed many wounded in this manner.

19

Church Services

No account of the war would be complete without some mention of the good work of the chaplains. They did their work nobly, and gave the greatest assistance to the bearers in getting the wounded down. I came into contact chiefly with those belonging to our own Brigade. Colonel Green, Colonel Wray, and Captain Gillitson; the latter was killed while trying to get one of our men who had been wounded. Services were held whenever possible, and sometimes under very peculiar circumstances. Once service was being conducted in the gully when a platoon was observed coming down the opposite hill in a position exposed to rifle fire. The thoughts of the audience were at once distracted from what the Padre was expounding by the risk the platoon was running; and members of the congregation pointed out the folly of such conduct, emphasizing their remarks by all the adjectives in the Australian vocabulary. Suddenly a shell burst over the platoon and killed a few men. After the wounded had been cared for, the Padre regained the attention of his congregation and gave out the last verse of 'Praise God from Whom all blessings flow'. There was one man for whom I had a great admiration — a clergyman in civil life but a stretcher-bearer on the Peninsula — Private Greig McGregor. He belonged to the 1st Field Ambulance, and I frequently saw him. He always had a stretcher, either carrying a man or going for one, and in his odd moments he cared for the graves of those who were buried on Hell Spit. The neatness of many of them was due to his kindly thought. He gained the D.C.M., and richly deserved it.

All the graves were looked after by the departed one's chums. Each was adorned with the Corps' emblems: thus the Artillery used shell caps, the Army Medical Corps a Red Cross in stone, etc.

20

The Engineers

The Engineers did wonderfully good work, and to a layman their ingenuity was most marked. Piers were made out of all sorts of things; for instance, a boat would be sunk and used as a buttress, then planks put over it for a wharf. They built a very fine pier which was afterwards named Watson's. Again, the 'monkey' of a pile driver they erected was formed out of an unexploded shell from the *Goeben*. This warship, a German cruiser taken over by the Turks, was in the Sea of Marmora, and occasionally the Commander in a fit of German humour would fire a few shells over Gallipoli neck into the bay — a distance of about eight or nine miles. As soon as the *Goeben* began firing, one of our aeroplanes would go up, and shortly afterwards the *Queen Elizabeth* could be seen taking up a position on our side of the Peninsula, and loosing off. Whether she hit the *Goeben* or not we never heard. It was *Mafeesh*.

The Engineers also made miles upon miles

of roads and, furthermore, created the nucleus of a water storage. A number of large tanks from Egypt were placed high up on 'Pluggey's', whence the water was reticulated into the far distant gullies.

21

Turks Attack

One night in May the Turks made a fierce attack on us, apparently determined to carry out their oft-repeated threat of driving us into the sea. The shells just rained down over our gully, lighting up the dug-outs with each explosion. It was like Hell let loose. Word came up from the beach station that they were full of casualties and on getting down there one found that the situation had not been over-estimated. The whole beach was filled with stretchers, the only light being that from bursting shells. We worked hard all night operating and dressing, and when one had time to think, one's thoughts generally took the shape of wondering how the men were keeping the Turks off. It was useless to be sentimental, although many of my friends were amongst those injured; the work just had to be done in the best way possible.

One night a strong wind got up, just like our 'Southerly Busters', and in the middle of it all firing began on our left. I heard that the Turks nearly got into the trenches, but they were beaten off and rolled right round the position — passed on, as it were, from battalion to battalion.

It was very interesting to watch the warships bombarding Turkish positions. One ship, attacking Achi Baba, used to fire her broadside, and on the skyline six clouds would appear at regular intervals, for all the world like windmills. On another occasion I watched two ships bombarding the same hill a whole afternoon. One would think there was not a square yard left untouched, and each shot seemed to lift half the hill. Twenty minutes after they had ceased firing, a battery of guns came out from somewhere and fired in their turn. They must have been in a tunnel to have escaped that inferno. One day we were up on 'Pluggey's' while our beach was being shelled; at last the stack of ammunition caught fire and was blazing fiercely until some of the men got buckets and quenched the fire with sea water most courageously. Later a shell landed among a lot of dug-outs. There was quietness for a bit; then one man began scraping at the disturbed earth, then another; finally about six of them were shovelling earth away; at last a man appeared with his birthday suit for his only attire. He ran like a hare for the next gully, amid the yells of laughter of all who witnessed the occurrence. I think he had been swimming, and being disturbed by 'Beachy', had run for a dug-out only to be buried by the shell.

That was the extraordinary thing about our soldiers. Shelling might be severe and searching, but only if a man was hit was it taken seriously. In that case a yell went up for stretcher-bearers; if it was a narrow squeak, then he was only laughed at.

That beach at times was the most unhealthy place in the Peninsula. Men frequently said they would sooner go back to the trenches. One day we had five killed and twenty-five wounded. Yet, had Johnny Turk been aware of it, he could have made the place quite untenable. I saw one shell get seven men who were standing in a group. The effect was remarkable. All screwed themselves up before falling. They were all lightly wounded.

22

Red Cross

About the middle of July I sent a corporal and two men over to Heliopolis with a letter to Lieutenant-Colonel Barrett, asking for some Red Cross goods. I had already received issue vouchers for two lots, but these had been intercepted in transit, so the men were ordered to sit on the cases until they gave delivery to the Ambulance. Fifty cases came, filled with pyjamas, socks, shirts, soap and all sorts of things. The day they arrived was very, very hot, and our hospital was full of men whose uniform had not been off since they landed. No time was lost in getting into the pyjamas, and the contented look on the men's faces would have gratified the ladies who worked so hard for the Red Cross. Talk about peace and contentment — they simply lolled about in the scrub smoking cigarettes, and I don't believe they would have changed places with a Federal Senator.

Those Red Cross goods saved one man's life at least. All the unopened cases were placed outside the tent. One afternoon a shell came over into a case of jam, went through it, and then into another containing socks. A man was lying under the shelter of this box, but the socks persuaded the shell to stay with them, and thus his life was saved. It was on this day that my nephew, Staff-Sergeant Nickson, was wounded. He had just left his dug-out to go to the dressing station on the beach when a shrapnel shell severely wounded him in the leg. The same shell killed Staff-Sergeant Gordon, a solicitor from Adelaide, and one of the finest characters I knew. He was shot through the spine and killed instantly. Two other men were wounded.

Our Ambulance was ordered to pitch a hospital up Canterbury Gully to provide for a possible outbreak of cholera, as almost every writer on the subject stated that, when European troops occupied trenches that had been previously held by Turks, an outbreak of cholera invariably followed. Major Clayton was detailed for the work, and soon had accommodation for a hundred men. As there was no cholera, the sick men were kept here. We had been so long in this place without a change, and so many troops were crowded into such a small area, without a possibility of real rest, that the men began to get very stale. Sickness was prevalent, and this hospital seemed to help them a great deal. It was a picture to see them all lying in their pyjamas reading the *Bulletin* and *Punch*, and swapping lies.

The New Zealanders held a concert here one night. Major Johnston, the O.C., filled the position of chairman, the chair being a cask. One man with a cornet proved a good performer; several others sang, while some gave recitations. We all sat round in various places in the gully, and joined in the choruses. It was very enjoyable while it lasted; but, as darkness came on, rifle-fire began on the tops of the surrounding hills — also, occasionally, shell fire. This completely drowned the sound of the performers' voices, and the concert had to be brought to a close; Abdul had counted us out.

23

Preparing for the Advance

Towards the end of July great preparations were made for an offensive movement, the object being to take Hill 971 and so turn the Turks' right. Large platforms were dug out of the hillsides in Monash Gully, each capable of holding three to five hundred men; they were constructed well below the sky line, and were fairly secure from shell fire. On these the incoming battalions were placed. There was not much room for sleep, but the main object seemed to be to have as many men handy as possible. The Turks seemed to be aware of the influx of troops, as they shelled the whole position almost all night. The beach, of course, was attended to most fervently, but considering the numbers of men landing few casualties occurred.

A 4.7 naval gun, which, I understand, had served in the relief of Ladysmith, was swathed in bags and landed on a barge, which conveyed it to a position alongside the pier. A party was put on to make a shield on the pier of boxes of our faithful friends the 'forty-niners', in case there were any Turks of an enquiring turn of mind along the beach towards Suvla.

The Engineers then constructed a landing place, and the gun was hauled ashore, again covered up, and conveyed to its position on our right during the night. General Birdwood outwitted the Turks that time, as they did not fire a shot during the whole operation.

On the third of August we received orders to remove to the left flank, the right being held by the Australian Division which participated in the operation known afterwards as Lone Pine. The last day on the beach proved to be pretty hot with shelling, chiefly from Beachy Bill. A number of pinnaces were busy all day towing in barges from the transports, and this could be easily seen from the olive grove where Bill had his lair. At one time the shells came over like rain; two of the pinnaces were hit below the water-line, and were in imminent danger of sinking. Through all the shelling Commander Cater ran along the pier to give some direction regarding the pinnaces, but was killed before he got there. He was a brave man, and always very courteous and considerate.

Our casualties during this afternoon were pretty considerable, and our stretcher-bearers were constantly on the 'go' getting men under shelter.

Early in the morning the Ghurkas came ashore, but the Turks spotted them, and gave them a cordial welcome to Anzac. They are a small-sized set of men, very dark (almost black), with Mongol type of face and very stolid. One was killed while landing. They were evidently not accustomed to shell-fire, and at first were rather scared, but were soon reassured when we told them where to stand in safety. Each carried in addition to his rifle a Kukri — a heavy, sharp knife, shaped something like a reaping-hook, though with a curve not quite so pronounced. It was carried in a leather case, and was as keen as a razor. I believe the Ghurkas' particular delight is to use it in lopping off arms at the shoulder-joint. As events turned out we were to see a good deal of these little chaps, and to appreciate their fighting qualities.

The 2nd Field Ambulance was to take our position on the beach. We packed up our panniers and prepared to leave the spot where we had done so much work during the last three months, and where we had been the unwilling recipients of so much attention from Beachy Bill and his friend Windy Annie. Our donkeys carried the panniers, and each man took his own wardrobe. Even in a place like this one collects rubbish, just as at home, and one had to choose just what he required to take away; in some cases this was very little, for each had to be his own beast of burden. Still, with our needs reduced to the minimum, we looked rather like walking Christmas-trees. The distance to Rest Gully was about a mile and a half, through saps and over very rough cobble-stones, and our household goods and chattels became heavy indeed before we halted; I know mine did.

24

The Attempt on Sari Bair

Our Ambulance was attached to the Left Assaulting Column, which consisted of the 29th Indian Brigade, 4th Australian Infantry Brigade, Mountain Battery and one company of New Zealand Engineers under Brigadier-General Cox.

The commanding officers of all the ambulances in General Godley's Division met in the gully and had the operation orders explained to them by the A.D.M.S. of the Division, Colonel Manders, a very capable officer. To my great regret he was killed two days later; we had been acquainted for some time, and I had a great regard for him.

The 4th Infantry Brigade was to operate in what was known as the Aghyl Dere ('Dere' in Turkish means 'gully'). The operation order gave out that we were to establish our Field Hospital in such a position as to be readily accessible for the great number of wounded we expected. Meantime, after making all arrangements for the move and ascertaining that each man knew his job exactly, we sat about for a while. The bombardment was to commence at 5 p.m. Precisely at that hour the *Bacchante* opened fire, the howitzers and our field guns co-operating, the Turks making a hearty response. The din was frightful. To make a man sitting beside me hear what I was saying, I had to shout at the top of my voice. However, there were not many men hit. We had tea — for which Walkley had got three eggs from somewhere, the first I had tasted since leaving Egypt. We tried to get some sleep, but that was impossible, the noise being so great; it was hard, too, to know where one was safe from bullets. Mr. Tute, the Quartermaster, and I got a dug-out fairly well up the hill, and turned in. We had not been long there when a machine-gun appeared to be trained right on to us — bullets were coming in quantities. It was pitch-dark, so we waited until they stopped, and then got further down the gully and tried to sleep there — but this particular dug-out had more than ourselves in it, and we passed the night hunting for things. The Division started to march out just after dark, the 4th Brigade leading. It was almost daylight before the rear of the column passed the place at which we were waiting. The men were all in great spirits, laughing and chaffing and giving the usual 'Are we down' earted?'. I think those men would laugh if they were going to be hanged. Our bearer divisions, in charge respectively of Captains Welch, Jeffries and Kenny, followed in rear of the Brigade, while the tent divisions came in rear of the whole column.

Major Meikle and I had often, like Moses viewing the Land of Promise, looked at the country over which the fight was now to take place — a stretch of flats about three miles long, from the beach up to the foot of the hills. As the day broke, we found a transformation at Nibronesi Point, which is the southernmost part of Suvla Bay. At nightfall not a ship was there; now there was a perfect forest of masts. The place looked like Siberia in Newcastle when there was a strike on. I counted ten transports, seven battle-cruisers, fourteen destroyers, twelve trawlers and a lot of pinnaces. These had landed the force which was afterwards known as the Suvla Bay Army. A balloon ship and five hospital ships were also at anchor in the bay. As we passed what was known as our No. 3 Outpost, we came across evidences of the fight — dead men, dead mules, equipment, ammunition boxes and rifles lying all over the place. We noted, too, little hillocks of sand here and there, from behind which the Turks had fired at our column. It was evident that our men had soon got in touch with the enemy and had driven him back. The Aghyl Dere proved to be a fairly wide gully with steep hills on either side. A little distance, about three quarters of a mile up, we came to what had been the Turkish Brigade Headquarters. Here everything was as they had left it. The surprise had been complete, and we had given them very short notice to quit. Clothing, rifles, equipment, copper pans and boilers were in abundance, and it was evident that Abdul makes war with regard to every comfort, for there were visible also sundry articles of wearing apparel only used by the gentler sex. The men had comfortable bivouacs and plenty of bed-clothing of various patterns. The camp was situated in a hollow, round in shape and about a hundred yards in diameter, with dug-outs in the surrounding hillsides; all was very clean, except for the fleas, of which a good assortment remained. The dug-outs were roofed in with waterproof sheets, buttoned together and held up by pegs which fitted into one another. These sheets, with the poles, made handy bivouac shelters, easily pitched and struck. Altogether, their camp equipment was better than ours.

We annexed all the pans and boilers and made good use of them for our own

Ambulance. Then, proceeding further up the gully, we found it almost impassable by reason of dead Ghurkas and mules; a gun on a ridge had the range of this place to a nicety, and the ammunition train was held up for a time. I never saw such a mess of entangled mules; they were kicking and squealing, many of them were wounded, and through it all the Indian drivers were endeavouring to restore some kind of order. One had to keep close under the banks to escape the shells. Not far from here was the emplacement of our old friend 'Windy Annie', but alas! Annie was constant to Abdul, and they had taken her with them. It was a great pity we did not get the gun. No wonder our guns never found the place. The ground had been dug out to some depth and then roofed over with great logs and covered with earth and sandbags; the ammunition — plenty of it — was in deep pits on either side; artillery quarters were in close proximity, and the tracks of the gun were clearly seen.

The shelling was far too heavy to let us pitch a dressing station anywhere here, so we retired to the beach to find a place more sheltered under the hills; the bearers meanwhile followed the troops. Soon scores of casualties began to arrive, and we selected a position in a dry creek about six yards wide, with high banks on either side. The operating tent was used as a protection from the sun and stretched from bank to bank, the centre being upheld by rifles lashed together; the panniers were used to form the operating table, and our drugs were placed round the banks. We were, however, much handicapped by not having any transport, as our donkeys had been requisitioned by the Army Service Corps. Everything had to be carried from a distance, and water was exceedingly scarce. All day we were treating cases and operating until late at night. Major Meikle and I divided the night, and we were kept going. From one until four in the morning I slept in a hole in a trench like a tomb.

At daylight we could see our men righting their way through the scrub over Sari Bair, the warships firing just ahead of them to clear the scrub of the Turkish Infantry. The foremost men carried flags, which denoted the farthest point reached and the extent of the two flanks, as a direction to the ship. With the glasses one could see that the bayonet was being used pretty freely; the Turks were making a great stand, and we were losing a lot of men. They could be seen falling everywhere.

25

Ambulance Work

Our bearers were doing splendid work; it was a long and dangerous carry, and a lot of them were wounded themselves. The miserable part of the affair was that the Casualty Clearing Station on the beach broke down and could not evacuate our wounded. This caused a block, and we had numbers of wounded on our hands. A block of a few hours can be dealt with, but when it is impossible to get cases away for forty hours the condition of the men is very miserable. However, we got the cooks going, and had plenty of Bovril and Oxo, which we boiled up with biscuits broken small. It made a very sustaining meal, but caused thirst, which was troublesome, as it was particularly difficult to obtain water. Shelter from the sun, too, was hard to get; the day was exceedingly hot, and there were only a few trees about. As many as could be got into the shade were put there, but we had to keep moving them round to avoid the sun. Many of the cases were desperate, but they uttered not a word of complaint — they all seemed to understand that it was not our fault that they were kept here.

As the cases were treated by us, they were taken down towards the beach and kept under cover as much as possible. At one time we had nearly four hundred waiting for removal to the ship. Then came a message asking for more stretchers to be sent to the firing line, and none were to be obtained; so we just had to remove the wounded from those we had, lay them on the ground, and send the stretchers up. Thank goodness, we had plenty of morphia, and the hypodermic syringe relieved many who would otherwise have suffered great agony.

Going through the cases, I found one man who had his arm shattered and a large wound in his chest. Amputation at the shoulder-joint was the only way of saving his life. Major Clayton gave the anaesthetic, and we got him through.

Quite a number of Ghurkas and Sikhs were amongst the wounded, and they all seemed to think that it was part of the game; patience loomed large among their virtues. Turkish wounded were also on our hands, and, though they could not speak our language, still they expressed gratitude with their eyes. One of the Turks was interrogated, first by the Turkish interpreter with no result; the Frenchman then had a go at him, and still nothing could be got out of him. After these two had finished, Captain Jefferies went over to the man and said, 'Would you like a drink of water?' 'Yes, please,' was the reply.

During one afternoon, after we had been in this place for three days, a battalion crossed the ground between us and the beach. This brought the Turkish guns into action immediately, and we got the time of our lives. We had reached a stage when we regarded ourselves as fair judges of decent shell-fire, and could give an unbiassed opinion on the point, but — to paraphrase Kipling — what we knew before was 'Pop' to what we now had to swallow. The shells simply rained on us, shrapnel all the time; of course our tent was no protection as it consisted simply of canvas, and the only thing to do was to keep under the banks as much as possible. We were jammed full of wounded in no time. Men rushing into the gully one after another, and even a company of infantry tried to take shelter there; but that, of course, could not be allowed. We had our Geneva Cross flag up, and their coming there only drew fire.

In three-quarters of an hour we put through fifty-four cases. Many bearers were hit, and McGowen and Threlfall of the 1st Light Horse Field Ambulance were killed.

Seven of our tent division were wounded. One man reported to me that he had been sent as a reinforcement, had been through Samoa, and had just arrived in Gallipoli. While he was speaking, he sank quietly down without a sound. A bullet had come over my shoulder into his heart. That was another instance of the fortune of war. Many men were hit, either before they landed or soon after, while others could go months with never a scratch. From 2 till 7 p.m. we dealt with 142 cases.

This shelling lasted for an hour or more, and when it subsided a party of men arrived with a message from Divisional Headquarters. They had been instructed to remove as many of the Ambulance as were alive. Headquarters, it appears, had been watching the firing. We lost very little time in leaving, and for the night we dossed down in the scrub a mile further along the beach, where we were only exposed to the fire of spent bullets coming over the hills. Our fervent prayer was that we had said good-bye to shells.

The new position was very nice; it had been a farm — in fact the plough was still there, made of wood, no iron being used in its construction. Blackberries, olives, and wild thyme grew on the place, and also a kind of small melon. We did not eat any; we thought we were running enough risks already; but the cooks used the thyme to flavour the bovril, and it was a nice addition.

Not far from us something happened that was for all the world like an incident described by Zola in his 'Dèbacle', when during the bombardment before Sedan a man went on ploughing in a valley with a white horse, while an artillery duel continued over his head. Precisely the same thing occurred here — the only difference being that here a man persisted in looking after his cattle, while the guns were firing over his head.

Walkley and Betts proved ingenious craftsmen. They secured two wheels left by the Signalling Corps, and on these fastened a stretcher; out of a lot of the web equipment lying about they made a set of harness; two donkeys eventuated from somewhere, and with this conveyance quite a lot of transport was done. Water and rations were carried as well, and the saving to our men was great. Goodness knows the bearers were already sufficiently worked carrying wounded.

The *Bacchante* did some splendid firing, right into the trenches every time. With one shot, amongst the dust and earth, a Turk went up about thirty feet: arms and legs extended, his body revolving like a catherine wheel. One saw plenty of limbs go up at different times, but this was the only time when I saw a man go aloft *in extenso*.

It was while we were in this position that W.O. Henderson was hit; the bullet came through the tent, through another man's arm and into Mr. Henderson. He was a serious loss to the Ambulance, as since its inception he had had sole charge of everything connected with the supply of drugs and dressings, and I missed his services very much.

We were now being kept very busy and had little time for rest, numbers of cases being brought down. Our table was made of four biscuit boxes, on which were placed the stretchers. We had to be very sparing of water, as all had to be carried. The donkey conveyance was kept constantly employed. Whenever that party left we used to wonder whether they would return, for one part of the road was quite exposed to fire; but Betts and Walkley both pulled through.

One night I had just turned in at nine-thirty, when Captain Welch came up to say that a bad casualty had come in, and so many came in afterwards that it was three o'clock in the following morning before I had finished operating. While in the middle of the work I looked up and found G. Anschau holding the lantern. He belonged to the 1st Field Ambulance, but had come over to our side to give any assistance he could. He worked like a Trojan.

We still had our swim off the beach from this position. It will be a wonderful place for tourists after the war is over. For Australians particularly it will have an unbounded interest. The trenches where the men fought will be visible for a long time, and there will be trophies to be picked up for years to come. All along the flat land by the beach there are sufficient bullets to start a lead factory. Then searching among the gullies will give good results. We came across the Turkish Quartermaster's store, any quantity of coats and boots and bully beef. The latter was much more palatable than ours.

Our men had a novel way of fishing; they threw a bomb into the water, and the dead fish would either float and be caught or go to the bottom — in which case the water was so clear that they were easily seen. Wilson brought me two, something like a mackerel, that were delicious.

As there was still a good deal of delay in getting the cases off, our tent was brought over from Canterbury Gully and pitched on the beach; the cooks keeping the bovril and biscuits going. We could not maintain it there long, however, as the Turks' rifle-fire was too heavy, so the evacuation was all done from Walker's Ridge about two miles away. The Casualty Clearing Station here (the 16th) was a totally different proposition from the other one. Colonel Corkery was commanding officer, and knew his job. His command was exceedingly well administered, and there was no further occasion to fear any block in getting our wounded off.

Amongst the men who came in to be dressed was one wounded in the leg. The injury was a pretty bad one, though the bone was not fractured. The leg being uncovered, the man sat up to look at it. He exclaimed 'Eggs a cook! I thought it was only a scratch!'

Our bearers did great work here, Sergeant Baber being in charge and the guiding spirit amongst them. Carberry from Western Australia proved his worth in another manner. The 4th Brigade were some distance up the gully and greatly in want of water. Carberry seems to have the knack of divining, for he selected a spot where water was obtained after sinking. General Monash drew my attention to this, and Carberry was recommended for the D.C.M.

Early in August, soon after Colonel Manders was killed, I was promoted to his position as Assistant Director of Medical

Services, or, as it is usually written, A.D.M.S. On this I relinquished command of the 4th Field Ambulance, and though I appreciated the honour of the promotion yet I was sorry to leave the Ambulance. We had been together so long, and through so much, and every member of it was of such sterling worth, that when the order came for me to join Headquarters I must say that my joy was mingled with regret. Everyone — officers, non-commissioned officers and men — had all striven to do their level best, and had succeeded. With one or two exceptions it was our first experience on active service, but all went through their work like veterans. General Godley, in whose division we were, told me how pleased he was with the work of the Ambulance and how proud he was to have them in his command. The Honour list was quite sufficient to satisfy any man. We got one D.S.O., two D.C.M.s, and sixteen 'Mentioned in Despatches'. Many more deserved recognition, but then all can't get it.

Major Meikle took charge, and I am sure the same good work will be done under his command. Captain Dawson came over with me as D.A.D.M.S. He had been Adjutant from the start until the landing, when he 'handed over' to Captain Finn, D.S.O., who was the dentist. Major Clayton had charge of

C Section; Captains Welch, Jeffries and Kenny were the officers in charge of the Bearer Divisions. Jeffries and Kenny were both wounded. Captain B. Finn, of Perth, Western Australia, was a specialist in eye and ear diseases. Mr. Cosgrove was the Quartermaster, and Mr. Baber the Warrant Officer; Sergeant Baxter was the Sergeant Clerk. To mention any of the men individually would be invidious. They were as fine a set of men as one would desire to command. In fact, the whole Ambulance was a very happy family, all doing their bit and doing it well.

On the 21st of August an attack was made on what were known as the W Hills — so named from their resemblance to that letter of the alphabet. Seated on a hill one had a splendid view of the battle. First the Australians went forward over some open ground at a slow double with bayonets fixed, not firing a shot; the Turks gave them shrapnel and rifle-fire, but very few fell. They got right up to the first Turkish trench, when all the occupants turned out and retired with more speed than elegance. Still our men went on, taking a few prisoners and getting close to the hills, over which they disappeared from my view. Next, a battalion from Suvla came across as supports. The Turks meanwhile had got the range to a nicety; the shrapnel was bursting neatly and low and spreading beautifully — it was the best Turkish shooting I had seen. The battalion was rather badly cut up, but a second body came across in more open order than the others, and well under the control of their officers; they took advantage of cover, and did not lose so many men. The fight was more like those one sees in the illustrated papers than any hitherto — shells bursting, men falling, and bearers going out for the wounded. The position was gained and held, but there was plenty of work for the Ambulance.

There were very few horses on the Peninsula, and those few belonged to the Artillery. But at the time I speak of we had one attached to the New Zealand and Australian Headquarters, to be used by the despatch rider. Anzac, the Headquarters of General Birdwood, was about two and a half miles away; and, being a true Australian, the despatch-carrier declined to walk when he could ride, so he rode every day with despatches. Part of the journey had to be made across a position open to fire from Walker's Ridge. We used to watch for the man every day, and make bets whether he would be hit. Directly he entered the fire zone, he started as if he were riding in the Melbourne Cup, sitting low in the saddle, while the bullets kicked up dust all round him. One day the horse returned alone, and everyone thought the man had been hit at last; but in about an hour's time he walked in. The saddle had slipped, and he came off and rolled into a sap, whence he made his way to us on foot.

When going through the trenches it is not a disadvantage to be small of stature. It is not good form to put one's head over the sandbags; the Turks invariably objected, and even entered their protest against periscopes, which are very small in size. Numbers of observers were cut about the face and a few lost their eyes through the mirror at the top being smashed by a bullet. On one occasion I was in a trench which the men were making deeper. A rise in the bottom of it just enabled me, by standing on it, to peer through the loophole. On commending the man for leaving this lump, he replied, 'That's a dead Turk, sir!'

26

Artillery

Watching the Field Artillery firing is very interesting. I went one day with General Johnstone of the New Zealand Artillery to Major Standish's Battery, some distance out on the left, and the observing station was reached through a long sap. It was quite close to the Turks' trenches, close enough to see the men's faces. All directions were given by telephone, and an observer placed on another hill gave the result of the shot — whether under, over, or to the right or left. Errors were corrected and the order to fire again given, the target meanwhile being quite out of sight of the battery commander.

It was amusing to hear the heated arguments between the Artillery and Infantry, in which the latter frequently and vehemently asseverated that they 'could have taken the sanguinary place only our own Artillery fired on them'. They invariably supported these arguments by the production of pieces of shell which had 'blanky near put their Australian adjective lights out'. Of course the denials of the Artillery under these accusations were very emphatic; but the production of the shell-fragments was awkward evidence, and it was hard to prove an alibi.

The advent of the hospital ship *Maheno* resulted in a pleasant addition to our dietary, as the officers sent ashore some butter, fresh bread and a case of apples. The butter was the first I had tasted for four and a half months. The *Maheno* belonged to the Union Company, and had been fitted up as a hospital ship under the command of Colonel Collins. He was the essence of hospitality, and a meal on board there was a dream.

While we were away along the beach for a swim one afternoon, the Turks began shelling our quarters. It had not happened previously, and everyone thought we were out of range. The firing lasted for about an hour and a half. I fully expected that the whole place would be smashed. On the contrary, beyond a few mules and three men hit, nothing had happened, and there was little in the ground to show the effects of the firing. (I noticed the same with regard to the firing of the naval guns. They appeared to lift tons of earth, but when one traversed the position later very little alteration could be detected.) The Turks, however started at night again, and one shot almost buried me in my dug-out.

The number of transports that came in and out of Anzac while we were there was marvellous, and a great tribute to the British Navy. There is no question as to who is Mistress of the Sea. Occasionally we heard of one being torpedoed, but considering the number constantly going to and fro those lost were hardly noticeable. The *Southland* was torpedoed while we were in Gallipoli, and Major Millard (who was on board) told me that there was not the slightest confusion, and only one life was lost.

27

Turks as Fighters

One cannot conclude these reminiscences without paying a tribute to Abdul as a fighting man. All I know about him is in his favour. We have heard all about his atrocities and his perfidy and unspeakablenesses, but the men we met fought fairly and squarely; and as for atrocities it is always well to hear the other side of the question. At the beginning of the campaign it was commonly reported that the Turks mutilated our wounded. Now I believe that to be an unmitigated lie, probably given a start by men who had never set foot in the Peninsula — or who, if they did, had taken an early opportunity of departure. We were in a position to know whether any mutilation had occurred, and I certainly saw none. I believe that similar reports were existent among the Turks regarding us, and I formed that opinion from the attitude and behaviour of one of the prisoners when I went to dress his wound. He uttered most piteous cries and his conduct led me to believe that he thought he was to be ill-treated. I have mentioned before the class to which most of the prisoners were. They were always most grateful for any kindness shown them.

As to their sense of fair play, when the *Triumph* was sunk, they never fired on her — though I understand it would have been quite allowable directly the men set foot on another warship. Again, about a fortnight after the landing at Anzac, we tried to land a force at Gaba Tepe, but had to retire and leave our wounded. The Turks signalled us to bring them off, and then they never fired or abused the white flag. The third instance occurred on our left, when we made the advance in August. Our Ambulance was under a hill, and a howitzer battery took up a position just in front. The Turk *sent word* that either the Ambulance or the battery would have to move, otherwise they would be forced to fire on the Ambulance.

The shells we got on the beach could not be attributed to any disregard of the Red Cross, for they could not see the flag, and moreover the Ordnance was next to us, a thing utterly out of order, but unavoidable under the circumstances.

My career on the Peninsula came to a close at the end of September, when I fell ill and was put on the hospital ship. The same evening a very willing attack was put up by the Turk.

One had a good and most interesting view, as one was in perfect safety. The bursting shells in the darkness were very picturesque.

Prior to going off we had often discussed the pleasure of getting between sheets and into a decent bed — how one would curl up and enjoy it. But my first night under those conditions was spent in tossing about, without a wink of sleep. It was too quiet. Being accustomed to be lulled to sleep by the noise of six-inch guns from a destroyer going over my dug-out, I could now hear a pin drop, and it was far too quiet. We found we were to be sent to England. Malta was no place in which to get rid of Mediterranean fever. The treatment the people of England give the Australians is handsome in the extreme. They cannot do enough to make them comfortable. Country houses are thrown open to the invalided men, perfect strangers though they are, and all are welcome.

Together with Major Courtenay (with whom I came over) I was taken to Lockleys, in Hertfordshire. Sir Evelyn and Lady de La Rue had a standing invitation at Horseferry Road, the Australian Military Headquarters, for six officers. We happened to be among the lucky ones to be included, and the kindness I received from our host and hostess will be remembered during the remainder of my life.

We do hope that you have enjoyed reading this large print book.

Did you know that all of our titles are available for purchase?

We publish a wide range of high quality large print books including:
Romances, Mysteries, Classics
General Fiction
Non Fiction and Westerns

Special interest titles available in large print are:
The Little Oxford Dictionary
Music Book
Song Book
Hymn Book
Service Book

Also available from us courtesy of Oxford University Press:
Young Readers' Dictionary
(large print edition)
Young Readers' Thesaurus
(large print edition)

For further information or a free brochure, please contact us at:
Ulverscroft Large Print Books Ltd.,
The Green, Bradgate Road, Anstey,
Leicester, LE7 7FU, England.
Tel: (00 44) 0116 236 4325
Fax: (00 44) 0116 234 0205

Other titles published by Ulverscroft:

GREY GRANITE

Lewis Grassic Gibbon

Widowed once again, Chris Colquohon has come to the industrial town of Duncairn, where life is as hard as the granite of the buildings all around her, and she must make her living as best she can by working in Ma Cleghorn's boarding house. Meanwhile, her son Ewan, forsaking his college career, finds employment at a steel manufacturer's, and determines to lead a peaceful strike against the manufacture of armaments. In the face of violence and police brutality, his socialist idealism is forged into something harder and fiercer as he readies himself to sacrifice all for the cause . . .

A TANGLED WEB

L. M. Montgomery

It all begins with Great Aunt Becky and her infamous prized possession: a legendary heirloom jug. After her death, everyone wants it. But the name of the new owner will not be revealed for one year . . . Over the next twelve months, scandals, quarrels and love affairs abound within the Dark and Penhallow clans — with the jug at the centre of it all. Engagements are broken; lifelong mutual hatred blossoms into romance; lovers separated years ago are reunited. But then comes the night that the eccentric matriarch's wishes will be revealed — and both families are in for the biggest surprise of them all.

VICE VERSA

F. Anstey

Mr. Bultitude is unmoved by the pleading of his fourteen-year-old son Dick that he be spared from returning to Grimstone's tortuous boarding school. During his harangue on the free and easy life of youth, Mr. Bultitude unwisely expresses the wish that he himself might be a boy again — whilst clutching the magical Garudâ Stone, which is all too ready to oblige by transforming his outward appearance into that of his son's. To add insult to injury, Dick swiftly seizes the stone — and with it, the opportunity not only to assume his father's mature and portly form, but also gleefully pack Mr. Bultitude off to the hellish halls of Grimstone's . . .